Judy Moody
Around the World in 8½ Days

Megan McDonald is the award-winning author of the Judy Moody series. She says that most of Judy's stories "grew out of anecdotes about growing up with my four sisters". She confesses, "I am Judy Moody. Same-same! In my family of sisters, we're famous for exaggeration. Judy Moody is me … exaggerated." Megan McDonald lives with her husband in northern California.

You can find out more about Megan McDonald and her books at **www.meganmcdonald.net**

Peter H. Reynolds says he felt an immediate connection to Judy Moody because "having a daughter, I hav̶ ̶ ̶ ̶ ̶ ̶ ̶ ̶ ̶ ̶ ̶ ̶ ̶ first hand the adventures of a ver̶ ̶ ̶ ̶ ̶ ̶ ̶ ̶ ̶ ̶ ̶ ̶ ̶ ̶ ̶. Peter H. Reynolds ̶ ̶ ̶ ̶ ̶ ̶ ̶ ̶ ̶ ̶ ̶ ̶ ̶ ̶ down the road ̶ ̶ ̶ ̶ ̶ ̶

You can find out m̶ ̶ ̶ ̶ ̶ ̶ ̶ ̶ ̶ Peter H. Reynolds and his art at **www.fablevision.com**

Books by Megan McDonald
and Peter H. Reynolds

Judy Moody
Judy Moody Gets Famous!
Judy Moody Saves the World!
Judy Moody Predicts the Future
Judy Moody: The Doctor Is In!
Judy Moody Declares Independence!
Judy Moody: Around the World in 8 1/2 Days
Judy Moody Goes to College
Judy Moody, Girl Detective
The Judy Moody Mood Journal
Judy Moody's Double-Rare Way-Not-Boring
Book of Fun Stuff to Do
Judy Moody's Way Wacky Uber Awesome
Book of More Fun Stuff to Do
Stink: The Incredible Shrinking Kid
Stink and the Incredible Super-Galactic Jawbreaker
Stink and the World's Worst Super-Stinky Sneakers
Stink and the Great Guinea Pig Express
Stink: Solar System Superhero
Stink and the Ultimate Thumb-Wrestling Smackdown
Stink-O-Pedia: Super Stink-y Stuff from A to Zzzzz
Judy Moody & Stink: The Holly Joliday
Judy Moody & Stink: The Mad, Mad, Mad,
Mad Treasure Hunt

Books by Megan McDonald
Ant and Honey Bee: What a Pair!
The Sisters Club
The Sisters Club: Rule of Three
The Sisters Club: Cloudy with a Chance of Boys

Books by Peter H. Reynolds
The Dot • Ish • So Few of Me

Judy Moody

Around the World in 8½ Days

Megan McDonald

illustrated by

Peter H. Reynolds

WALKER
BOOKS

First published 2007 by Walker Books Ltd
87 Vauxhall Walk, London SE11 5HJ

This edition published 2011

30

Text © 2006 Megan McDonald
Illustrations © 2006 Peter H. Reynolds
Judy Moody font © 2003 Peter H. Reynolds

The right of Megan McDonald and Peter H. Reynolds to be identified as
author and illustrator respectively of this work has been asserted by them
in accordance with the Copyright, Designs and Patents Act 1988

Judy Moody™. Judy Moody is a registered trademark
of Candlewick Press Inc., Somerville MA

This book has been typeset in Stone Informal

Printed and bound in Great Britain by Clays Ltd, St Ives plc

British Library Cataloguing in Publication Data:
a catalogue record for this book
is available from the British Library

ISBN 978-1-4063-3588-0

www.walker.co.uk

For the tarantella dancers
of Girl Scout Troop #997
M. M.

To my brothers and sisters,
Andrew, Jane, Paul, and Renee —
all born around the world
P. H. R.

Table of Contents

Judy Moody

Way-official card-carrying
member of the
My-Name-Is-a-Poem Club

Dad

One-of-a-kind Dad

Mum

One-and-only Mum

Nellie Bly

Daredevil reporter.
Raced around the world
in 72 days, 6 hours,
11 minutes, 14 seconds

Who's

Who

Stink
Stink McFink,
fratellino, bratellino

Frank
Frank the Prank,
aka Earl the Pearl

Rocky
Rocky No-Talky

Amy Namey
Amy Same-Samey,
gum-chewing girl reporter

Rhyme Time

The girl had a notebook and a clipboard. The girl wore a blue plaid skirt, like a school uniform, and not one but TWO watches. The girl had a pencil behind her ear. The girl was very noticeable in her blue-green glasses.

The girl came over to Judy Moody's lunch table and plopped herself down in between Judy's friends Rocky and Frank.

She, NOT Judy Moody, looked like she was in a reporter mood.

Who was this important-looking, glasses-wearing girl anyway, Judy wondered.

"Amy Namey, Girl Reporter," said the girl. "What's the scoop?"

"Um … Screamin' Mimi's chocolate mud?" asked Judy.

"Not the ice cream kind of scoop," said the girl. "The story kind of scoop. I'm a reporter," she said. "Like Nellie Bly, Dare-devil Reporter."

She, Judy Moody, could not believe her ears.

Frank asked, "Is that like Elizabeth Blackwell, First Woman Doctor?"

Judy leaned in closer.

"Check!" said the girl. She wrote something on her clipboard. "I'm from Ms Valentine's class, 3V. Can I ask you a few questions? For my newspaper?"

"You've got your own paper?" asked Frank Pearl.

"Sure!" said the girl. Just then, Super-Important Girl Reporter held out a ketchup-bottle microphone.

"What's your favourite school lunch?" she asked. "Hawaiian pizza, southern fried chicken, or French toast?"

"French toast is *breakfast*," said Judy.

"Pizza!" screamed Rocky and Frank at the same time.

"Check!" said the girl. She ticked the list on her clipboard.

"I bring packed lunch," said Judy.

"How many times a week should the canteen have pizza?" she asked.

"Three," said Frank.

"Five!" said Rocky. "Every day! With extra cheese!"

"Check!" said the girl.

Who was this list-ticking, clipboard-carrying Pizza Reporter, anyway? And why were Rocky and Frank, Judy's best-ever friends, talking to her?

"You can't really get us pizza for lunch every day," said Judy.

"Why not?" asked the girl. "My mum

knows the dinner ladies. Besides, it's a free country."

"Hey! That's what *you* always say!" Frank said to Judy.

"Do not!"

"Do too!" said Rocky and Frank at the same time.

"Question Number Three," said the girl. "What else would you like to change about Virginia Dare School?"

"Snack machines!" said Frank.

"A swimming pool!" said Rocky.

"A skate park!" said Frank.

"No School Photo Day!" said Rocky. Girl Reporter was writing as fast as they could talk.

"No Pizza Reporters bugging us at lunchtime," said Judy. The girl stopped writing. The girl did not say "Check!".

In spite of herself, Judy got caught up in the moment. "OK. I have an idea! For real!" said Judy. "Chewing gum in school!"

"Yep," said Rocky.

"Yes!" said Frank.

"Check!" said the girl.

"I could work on my ABC gum collection at school," said Judy. "Start one under my desk. Not just at home on the lamp by my bed."

Girl Reporter was writing again.

"*ABC* stands for *Already Been Chewed*," said Judy.

"I know that," said the girl. "I collect gum too. I've been to see the world's best-ever collection of ABC gum. The biggest in the world."

"Huh?" asked Judy.

"Sure!" said the girl. "Bubblegum Alley. It's in California."

"I went to Boston," said Judy.

"I went there during the summer holidays. You walk down this alley between two buildings and there's a Wall of Gum on each side. Chewed-up gum that people stuck there. Some people have even made pictures and stuff out of gum. I chewed five black gumballs from the machine they have there and added it to the wall."

"No way!" said Rocky.

"Way!" said the girl. "It's like a Gum Hall of Fame. Or a Gum *Wall* of Fame." The girl cracked herself up.

"Double cool!" said Frank.

"I sent away for a Make-Your-Own-Gum Kit," said Judy. Nobody said a word.

"I'd really like to see a *Wall* of Gum!" said Frank.

"I have a picture of me standing in front of it," said the girl. "It was in the last issue of my paper. See?" She pulled out a page from the back of the clipboard.

WALL OF GUM

"Whoa!" said Rocky. "Weird. Look at all that chewed-up gum!"

"Wow," said Frank. "You really were there!"

"I had my picture in the *real* newspaper once," said Judy.

"Yeah, your *elbow*," said Rocky. Frank and Rocky cracked up.

"Thanks for your ideas," said the girl. "I've got to go and talk to Mr Todd."

"Mr Todd? That's *our* teacher," said Judy.

"I know. He has a big scoop for me."

"We already know he's getting married," said Judy.

"She tries to predict the future," Rocky explained.

"And once she predicted Mr Todd was getting married. And he is!" Frank announced.

"Wow!" said the girl. "That's a good scoop!" Judy sat up taller.

"Do real reporters wear pencils behind their ears?" asked Frank.

"Check!" said the girl. She looked at both of her watches. "Later, alligators!" she called, tucking the pencil behind her ear.

"Wow!" said Frank. "That girl is just like you, Judy!"

"Nah-uh," said Judy.

"Yah-huh!" said Rocky and Frank together.

"You're like twins or something," said Frank.

"Two of a kind," said Rocky.

"Name one thing the same," said Judy.

Judy Moody. Amy Namey

"Amy Namey. Judy Moody. Her name rhymes. Your name rhymes. Same-same!" said Frank.

"So? She has long, not-messy hair and dimples. And she wears glasses," said Judy. "I don't wear glasses."

"She dresses up like Some Lady, First Woman Reporter," said Rocky.

"I only dressed up like Elizabeth Blackwell, First Woman Doctor, once."

"And she collects ABC gum and likes getting her picture in the paper," said Frank.

"And don't forget she gets scoops," said Rocky, "which is like trying to predict the future."

"She probably likes Band-Aids and pizza tables, too," said Frank. "We should ask her."

"And she says weird stuff like 'check' all the time," Rocky added.

"I do not say weird stuff all the time," Judy protested.

"It's like they took a machine and made a copy," said Rocky.

"Maybe she's your clone!" said Frank.

"ROAR!" said Judy.

She, Judy Moody, liked being one of a kind. An original. Her mum said she was unique. Her dad said she was an individual. Mr Todd said she was in a class of her own (even though there were twenty other kids in Class 3T!).

Being unique made Judy feel special. That's the way it is, was, and always would be. *Should* be.

Until now. Until Amy Namey, Gum-Chewing Girl Reporter, moved in.

Now she felt like a NOT-one-of-a-kind, machine-made copy. A two-of-a-kind, un-original, boring old not-stand-alone clone.

Heebie-Jeebies

Judy was helping Stink with his homework, quizzing him for a science test.

"Name the four seasons," said Judy.

"Easy. Salt, pepper, ketchup and mustard," said Stink.

"Seasons of the YEAR, Stink," said Judy. "Never mind. How about this one. What makes dew form?"

"When leaves sweat?" asked Stink.

"N-O!" said Judy. "Here's one. You have to know *this*. What is a fibula?"

"Oh, I know. That's like when you tell a lie, but not a really big one. A little one."

"No, Stink. It's a bone! In your leg! Between your knee and your ankle. I think you'd better study some more. Now, can I ask you a question?"

"I thought that's what you *were* doing."

"Not a science test question. What would you do if you thought there was just one Stink, then you found out there was somebody else out there just like you? Like another Stink?"

"I'd bug you TWICE as much."

"Never mind. I'll ask Mum and Dad."

Judy asked her mum. Mum just hugged her and said, "You're the one and only Judy Moody in my book."

"Is this for science? Or social studies?" asked Dad.

"You don't understand," Judy told her dad. "There's only ONE of you and ONE of Mum and ONE of Stink. But, well, I mean, what if you met somebody and they were just like you? And you didn't feel special any more?"

"At least I'd have a new best friend," said Dad.

Hmmm. Judy thought about that one. Best friend? Or best enemy?

The next day, Best-Enemy Girl Reporter came up to Judy at breaktime. "Hi! Remember me?"

"Check," said Judy, frowning.

"You do remember! Your name's Judy.

Right? What's your last name? I want to put your chewing-gum-at-school idea in my paper."

Judy perked up. "Moody. Judy Moody."

"Judy Moody? For real? Hey, you rhyme! Just like me!"

"Same-same," said Judy excitedly.

"So, do kids always try to rhyme stuff with you? Like 'Amy Namey, how's Jamie? Want to play a game-y? You're so lame-y'. Stuff like that?"

"I've heard 'Howdy Doody, Judy Moody' and 'Judy Moody has cooties' about ten hundred million times!"

"Exactly! It's so cool we both have the rhyming name thing. You could be in my club."

"I'm already in a club. The Toad Pee Club. With my friends."

"But this is a real club. It's not for just anybody. It's for people all over the world with names that rhyme. It's called the My-Name-Is-a-Poem Club."

"For real?" asked Judy.

"How real is this?" Amy reached into her pocket and pulled out a card. A way-official, real-and-true membership card.

My-Name-Is-A-Poem Club

Amy Namey is a card-carrying member of the INTERNATIONAL MY-NAME-IS-A-POEM CLUB

Signed,
Hugh Blue
PRESIDENT, UK BRANCH

"RARE!" said Judy. "You mean I could be a member? Of a club that has people in it from all over the whole world?"

"Sure! I can sign you up!"

"You mean I'd get a card like this? A real membership card with my name on it and everything?"

"Check!" said Amy.

"Wow," said Judy. "How come I never knew about you before?"

"Oh, I've been around," said Amy. "Around the world!" She cracked up.

"What stuff do you do in your club?" Judy asked.

"Mostly you just carry this card around. But you can write to anybody in the club.

And sometimes they write back and send you a postcard. With a cool stamp from another country and everything."

"Whoa!"

"I know! I get postcards from people around the world, like, let's see … Nancy Clancy, Newton Hooton, and Sing Ling. Even Mark Clark van Ark from Newark! That's in this country. In New Jersey."

"No way!"

"Uh-huh. I even got one from somebody named Heebie Jeebie."

"That gives me the heebie-jeebies."

"I think that one was a joke, for sure. But my favourite is the one I got from Chip Dippe."

"Like potato chips and dip?"

"Exactly." Judy and Amy cracked up.

"I want to do it!" said Judy. "I want to be in the club!"

"Great!" said Amy. "Why don't you come over to my house on Saturday morning? I'll get you a membership card and everything."

"I'll ask. Do I have to pay any money?" Judy asked.

"Nope. It's a freebie," said Amy.

"So I won't have to get the heebie-jeebies," said Judy.

"Nopey-dopey!" said Amy.

"Okey-dokey!" said Judy. They fell on the floor laughing.

Amy Namey was so clever. And funny. And important-looking in her glasses, with two watches, and a pencil behind her ear.

AND her name rhymed. AND she was a member of a way-cool, around-the-world club. AND she knew a top-secret scoop from Mr Todd.

Amy Namey had all the things that made a New Best Enemy into a New Best Friend.

Club Snub

The next day, before going to school, Judy rummaged through her top drawer, looking for her old purple watch. It still worked! She wore it right next to her new red striped one.

She looked around for a clipboard, but she couldn't find one. So she stuck a Grouchy pencil behind her ear and went to school.

"There's a pencil in your hair," said Rocky.

"I know," Judy said. "Amy Namey says I can help her with her newspaper. A good reporter should have a pencil ready at all times."

"How come you're wearing two watches?" asked Frank.

"All the better to tell the time with," said Judy in a Little-Red-Riding-Hood-and-the-Wolf voice.

"No, really," said Frank.

"Amy Namey has one watch that tells normal time, and one that tells France time. Just like Nellie Bly, Daredevil Reporter. Amy says Nellie Bly always had one watch set to the time it was at home in

New York. The other watch she changed to the time in England or Italy or France – wherever she was."

"Whatever," said Rocky.

"How come Amy's other watch is on France time?" asked Frank.

"I don't know," said Judy. "I'll just have to get the scoop, won't I?" She took the pencil from behind her ear and wrote herself a note. Just like a real reporter would. "Maybe I'll ask her when she comes to our class after morning break to tell us a top-secret scoop that only Mr Todd knows."

"Wait. She's coming here? To Mr Todd's room?" asked Rocky.

"She's not going to be in our class, is she?" asked Frank.

"No. She just has a big fat secret to tell us."

"How do you know?" Rocky asked.

"I know," said Judy. "Or ... maybe I can ask her when I *go over to her house* to have a meeting of our *new club*."

"What new club?" asked Rocky.

"What new club?" asked Frank.

"The My-Name-Is-a-Poem Club," said Judy.

"Can we be in the club?" asked Frank.

"It's for people *all over the world* who have names that rhyme. Like Judy Moody. Amy Namey. Hello! *Frank* does not rhyme with

Pearl. *Rocky* does not rhyme with *Zang*."

"That's not fair," said Rocky. "We can't help it if our names don't rhyme."

"I didn't make the rules," said Judy.

"What if I change my name to Earl? *Earl the Pearl* rhymes." Judy and Rocky cracked up.

"Then we'd have to call you Earl," said Rocky. "That would be weird."

"OK. So keep calling me Frank and come to the Toad Pee Club meeting on Saturday morning. Don't go to that rhyming girl's house."

"What do you mean?" asked Judy.

"Didn't Stink tell you? We're having a really big, important meeting of the Toad Pee Club," said Frank.

"How come?"

"We want to enter Toady in a race they're having at the pet shop that morning. Fur & Fangs. You can win a tarantula."

"Stink told you about it?" asked Judy.

"Uh-huh."

"It's a girl tarantula named Trudy," added Frank. "It's a painted tarantula and it has orange stripes."

"And it has eight eyes, and fangs, and it keeps away robbers," said Rocky.

"Robbers!" said Judy. "There aren't any robbers around here."

"Yah-huh. *Friend*-robbers," Rocky said. "Maybe it works on people who steal other people's friends, like Little Miss You-Know-Who."

"Well, sorry, but I have to go to my new club. Amy Namey says—"

"AmyNameyAmyNamey. That girl's all you talk about now," said Rocky.

"Amy Namey sounds lame-y if you ask me," said Frank.

"Ha! Amy Namey *said* you'd say that!" said Judy.

Rocky looked at Frank. Frank looked at Rocky and shrugged.

"What's wrong with you guys?" said Judy. "Yesterday you liked her."

"Yeah, and yesterday you *didn't* like her," said Rocky.

"Just because she rhymes," said Frank. "We were friends with you FIRST. Before Suzy New-Club came along."

"Yeah, along comes Amy Rhymey and you forget about us," Rocky said.

"I bet any money a toad never peed on her," said Frank. "So she can't be in OUR club. No way."

"Shh! Here she comes!" said Judy.

"*Bonjour!*" said Amy Namey. "That means 'hello' in France."

"Whatever," said Rocky.

"Hey, can we ask you a question?" asked Frank.

"OK, shoot," said Amy. "But hurry up.
I have to give a report to your class."

"Has a toad ever peed on you?" asked
Rocky.

"What? NO!" said Amy.

"See?" Rocky and Frank said to Judy.

Nellie Bly Says Goodbye

"Class!" said Mr Todd, flicking the lights on and off. "Breaktime is over. Everybody find a seat. We have a special visitor today. And she has some interesting information to share with us."

"Is it the Crayon Lady?" somebody asked.

"Is *that* the visitor?" asked Bradley, pointing to Amy Namey. "She's just a kid. From Ms Valentine's class."

"Class, I'd like you to meet Amy Namey," said Mr Todd. Some kids giggled when he said her name.

Judy practically jumped out of her seat. "I already know her!" she said. "And we have three connections. One, her name rhymes, just like Judy Moody. Two, she likes Nellie Bly, Daredevil Reporter, the way I like Elizabeth Blackwell, First Woman Doctor. Three, she collects ABC gum."

"Thank you, Judy. I was about to say that some of you may know Amy from 3V, Ms Valentine's class."

"She lives on my street," Alison S. told Mr Todd.

"I noticed your colourful glasses earlier," said Jessica Finch.

"Were you on our field trip to the hospital?" asked Samantha.

"Why are you always wearing that blue checked skirt?" asked Rocky.

"Why do you have that plastic bread bag full of stuff?" asked Frank.

"Let's give Amy a chance," said Mr Todd. "She's here to tell us about Nellie Bly, the daredevil reporter who went all the way around the world in seventy-two days."

"Did anybody ever see the movie *Around the World in Eighty Days*?" Amy asked. Only a few hands went up.

"Nellie Bly was a woman reporter,"

Amy continued. "She wrote stuff for news-papers. She read this book about Mr Fogg. He was a made-up person who went around the world in eighty days. Nellie thought it would be cool for a real person to try to beat his record. So her newspaper sent her around the world. Another reporter found out and tried to beat her. But Nellie won the race. She went around the world in seventy-two days, six hours, eleven minutes and fourteen seconds."

Amy Namey looked over at Mr Todd.

"You're doing really well!" said Mr Todd.

"Someday I want to be a reporter and travel around the world like Nellie Bly," said Amy.

"Why don't you tell us how Nellie Bly

got ready for her trip?" said Mr Todd.

"She only had three days to get ready to go around the whole entire world. And she could only take one small bag, the size of a loaf of bread." Amy held up her loaf-of-bread bag.

"Just think, class," said Mr Todd. "What if you had to go all the way around the world and you could only take what fits in this bag? What are some of the things you would take? Jessica?"

"A camera."

"Judy?"

"A Grouchy pencil."

"Bradley?"

"Clean underwear." Everybody cracked up.

"Jessica again?"

"My stuffed pig called Snuffles."

"Frank?"

"A burger. And my pillow."

"Your pillow's bigger than a loaf of bread," said Bradley.

"Rocky?"

"I'd fill that whole bag with money!"

"Amy, would you like to show us what's in your bag?"

"These are some things Nellie Bly had in *her* bag. Soap. Needle and thread. Pyjamas. Slippers."

"No pillow?" asked Frank.

"Underwear," said Amy.

"Told ya!" said Bradley.

"Ink and pens and pencils."

"I said that!" said Judy.

"Three hats, a cup, a raincoat —"

"No way!" everybody exclaimed. Amy unfolded a tiny pouch and it turned into a raincoat.

"Whoa!" Everybody oohed and aahed.

"And ... her lucky thumb ring."

Holy macaroni! thought Judy. Lucky thumb ring! A lucky thumb ring was almost as good as a mood ring.

"What about money?" asked Rocky.

"She tied it in a little bag around her neck."

"What about clothes and stuff?" asked Jessica Finch.

"She only wore one dress. It was blue plaid, like this skirt." Amy Namey pointed to the skirt she was wearing.

"What's the stick for?" somebody asked. "Why'd she take a stick?"

"When she got to a country called Yemen, she had to brush her teeth with a stick."

"I can't believe there's a country called Yeah Man!" said Frank.

"And she saw camels and people riding elephants, and when she was halfway around the world, she got a pet monkey called McGinty!"

"Amy, why don't you show us Nellie Bly's around-the-world route on your globe?" said Mr Todd.

"OK. I made a globe this morning. It's still a bit wet." She held up a big gloopy papier-mâché ball. "Here's where she started, in Hoboken."

"She started in Hobo Land?"

"Hoboken is in the United States," said Amy. "And she went to England, France, Italy. Then Egypt, in Africa." The route was marked in black marker pen. Amy traced it with her finger.

"Can somebody help me hold this?" asked Amy.

"I will!" said Frank.

"Me too," said Rocky.

Judy could not believe her ears. Ten minutes ago, Rocky and Frank were calling Amy a robber. A big fat friend-stealer.

Now they were helping her!

Frank held the papier-mâché globe. "Where's that Yeah Man place?" he asked.

"I can see it," said Rocky. He went over to the noticeboard and pulled out a drawing pin. "It's right down here, on the Red Sea." As he said it, he stuck the pin into the globe to mark the spot.

POW! A loud pop made everybody jump. Frank leaped backwards. It was the balloon inside the papier-mâché globe! All the air went out of the globe with a *whoosh,* and it collapsed in on itself.

Frank looked at Rocky. Rocky looked at Frank. "Globe explode!" Rocky said, cracking up.

Amy Namey stood in front of the whole entire Class 3T, holding a mushy, gushy mess of wet newspaper. A slobby-blobby, ooey-gluey globe of gloop.

"Nellie Bly says goodbye!" said Amy, and she rushed out of the room.

Bella Tarantella

Judy passed a note to Frank, who passed it to Rocky.

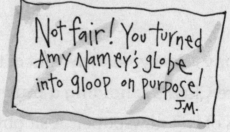

Rocky passed a note to Frank, who passed it to Judy.

Judy was about to pass another note when Mr Todd told the class it was time for the big scoop. She sat up straight as a pencil.

Mr Todd was drawing a map on the board. Judy hoped a map was not the big surprise.

"Class, we're about to start a whole new way of learning geography," Mr Todd announced. "Class 3T is going to go around the world in eight days!"

"What? Huh?" everybody asked.

"We're going to work with Ms Valentine's class—"

"Yippee!" said Judy. "That's Amy Namey's class." Rocky and Frank frowned at her.

"We'll make a big map like the one on the board and put it up in the corridor between our classrooms. Then we'll trace the journey of First Around-the-World Woman Reporter Nellie Bly. We'll learn about all the countries she visited."

"Did she go to Italy?" asked Rocky. "My grandma's from there."

"Yes," said Mr Todd.

"Did she go to Disneyland?" asked Bradley.

Mr Todd chuckled. "I'm afraid not." He wrote the names of eleven countries on the board.

"We'll get into small groups, and each group will take a country. Here are some

USA
ENGLAND
FRANCE
ITALY
EGYPT
YEMEN
SRI LANKA
MALAYSIA
SINGAPORE
CHINA
JAPAN

things you might try to find out about for each country."

Mr Todd pointed at the board:

A) WHAT THE FLAG LOOKS LIKE

B) TRADITIONAL FOOD FOR YOUR COUNTRY

C) HOW TO SAY HELLO AND GOODBYE
OR COUNT TO TEN IN YOUR
COUNTRY'S LANGUAGE

D) ANY GAMES THAT STARTED IN
YOUR COUNTRY

"We only have eight days to get all the way around the world, so we're going to have to work fast. There's a lot to learn, a lot to do."

"Can we bring in something real from that country?" asked Jessica Finch. "I have a set of dolls from Russia."

"I'm sorry. That's not one of the countries we're studying," said Mr Todd.

"I have money from Italy," said Rocky. "And some *carbone dolce*. It's a black sweet that looks like coal."

"Ooh, I have tea from London," said Judy. "That's in England. And I have a cuckoo clock in my bedroom that my grandma Lou brought me all the way from Germany."

"Tell you what," said Mr Todd. "These are all good ideas, but let's wait until you know what country you'll be working on."

"Is this the big scoop?" asked Frank. "Geography?"

"Yes," said Mr Todd. "I'm afraid it is. But I haven't told you the best part. We are going to kick off our Around-the-World tour with – a movie."

"Movie! What movie?" somebody asked.

"You mean we get to watch a movie at school?" asked Frank.

"Do we get to turn out the lights and eat popcorn?" asked Jessica Finch.

"We'll see," said Mr Todd. "The movie is *Around the World in Eighty Days*!"

"Yippee!" everybody yelled.

    ❧   ❧   ❧

That afternoon, the whole class got to go to Ms Valentine's room and watch the movie. Judy sat on the floor next to Amy Namey. They ate blue popcorn (made from blue corn!) and laughed at this inventor called Mr Fogg, who was trying to fly and flew right through a painting! And he was trying to race around the world in eighty days and some old men kept calling him a nincompoop!

After the movie, Judy went back to class and got into her small group with Rocky and Frank and Jessica Finch. They chose Italy for their project. They went to the library to look up some books on Italy.

"What's red, white and green all over?" asked Rocky.

"A Christmas elf?" asked Jessica.

"A pizza with green peppers?" asked Frank.

"No! The flag of Italy," said Rocky.

"Hey, that's funny!" said Judy. "We could start off with a joke like that."

"We could dress up in red, white and green," said Jessica.

"Yeah!" said Judy. "I love dressing up in crazy outfits!"

"OK," said Rocky and Frank.

"Let's definitely have pizza," said Rocky.

"Yeah, pizza!" said Frank.

"Let's think of something different," said Judy. "Everybody already knows about pizza."

"So? Pizza's the best!" said Rocky. "Italy without the pizza is like Judy without the Moody!"

"How about a pizza spelling test?" asked Jessica Finch. "We could spell words that are on pizza, like P-E-P-P-E-R-O-N-I."

"Not you too," said Judy.

"We could spell other stuff besides just pizza words," said Jessica. "Like *spaghetti, Parmesan* and *P-I-N-O-C-C-H-I-O*."

"Not even grown-ups can spell the word *Pinocchio*," said Rocky. "Everybody would flunk."

"We could make a Leaning Tower of Pizza!" said Frank.

"Out of what?" asked Judy.

"Pizza tables! You collect them," said Frank.

"Yeah, we could glue them all together into a tower," said Rocky.

"No way!" said Judy. "I'm not letting you go all glue-crazy on my whole collection. Stick to eating paste."

"Nobody's eating paste," said Rocky. "Just pizza."

"You guys have pizza on the brain," said Judy.

"Then let's hear your un-pizza brainy ideas," said Rocky.

Judy pointed to a picture in the book showing people dancing in a circle. "We could do this. Dance the tar-an-tell-a."

"I don't know how to dance," said Rocky.

"Especially the tarantula," said Frank.

Mr Todd passed by their table and saw the picture. "A dance from Italy is a very good idea," said Mr Todd. "*Bella Tarantella.*"

"See?" Judy grinned. "It's a very good idea."

"It'll take some practice," said Mr Todd. "But you'll get the hang of it."

"My grandma has an old record of that dance," said Rocky.

"Let's all go to Rocky's to practise," said Judy. "How about Saturday?"

"Can't!" said Rocky. "Frank and I will be at Fur & Fangs. Not like *some* people." He gave Judy the hairy eyeball.

"I meant Saturday *afternoon,*" said Judy. "I'll be back from Amy Namey's by then."

"I'd love to go to Rocky's on Saturday," said Jessica. "Sounds like fun."

"I don't know," said Frank. "The only

time I tried to dance was around the May-pole in the first year. I tripped and got all tangled up in streamers and ended up looking like a human candy cane."

"No human candy canes. We promise," said Judy.

"OK then, everybody. How about we meet at my house on Saturday at two o'clock?" Rocky said.

"C'mon, it'll be fun!" Judy elbowed Frank.

"Yeah, maybe if you're an eight-legged spider," said Frank.

Fratellino Bratellino

On Saturday morning, Dad agreed to take Judy to Amy Namey's house. Judy checked to make sure she had on BOTH of her watches. Her purple watch was set to normal time in Virginia. Her red striped watch was set to Italy time. And she wore her mood ring on her thumb so she could have a lucky thumb ring, just like Nellie Bly, Daredevil Reporter. *"Ciao, Mamma! Ciao, Stink!"*

"Why do you keep saying *chow*?" asked Stink. "Like it's time to eat or something."

"Or something! Don't have a cow, Stink. It's Italian," said Judy. "I'm learning words from Italy for our Around-the-World-in-Eight-Days project at school."

"You mean your Drive-Your-Family-

Crazy-in-Eight-Days project, don't you?" asked Stink. Mum and Dad laughed.

"N-O!" said Judy.

"Does *chow* mean 'hello' or 'goodbye'?" asked Stink.

"BOTH!" said Judy.

"Weird," said Stink. "'Hello' means 'goodbye' in Italy? What a country!"

"*Ciao, bambino,*" Judy said to Stink.

"*Bambino*? Isn't that a baby?" asked Stink. "I am not a baby!"

"OK, then, *ciao, fratellino.*"

"What's that?"

"'Little brother'. Wait, no. I'm wrong. Oh, yeah, I remember now. It's *BRATellino*!"

"Is not."

"Yah-huh! I mean, *sì,*" said Judy.

"How come you're wearing two watches?" asked Stink.

"You know how two heads are better than one?"

"Yeah. And two cuckoo clocks make you twice as cuckoo?"

"No," said Judy. "Two watches are better than one, too."

"Oh," said Stink. "Where are you going, anyway?"

"To Amy Namey's house."

"But what about the Toad Pee Club? This morning we're racing Toady at Fur & Fangs. I might win a tarantula."

"*Buona fortuna*," Judy said.

"What's tuna fish got to do with anything?" asked Stink.

"Nothing. It means 'good luck'," said Judy. "I don't know how to say 'buzz off' in Italian."

"But you're the one who always says Toady belongs to the whole Toad Pee Club, not just me. So we should all go. Together. That's what makes it a *club*."

"Stink, don't you get it? I'm in a new club now. And today I'm going to get my own way-official, real-and-true member-ship card. For sure and absolute positive."

"What club? Can I be in it? I want a way-official membership card too."

"It's the My-Name-Is-a-Poem Club, Stink. Sorry. It's only for people who have a name that rhymes. So unless you changed your name to Stink McFink —"

"I don't care. I'll be Stink McFink," said Stink.

"No way, Stink McNay. No dice, Stink McLice. No go, *bratellino*." Judy cracked herself up all the way to the car.

Addresses and Messes

"*Ciao!*" Judy said to Amy.

"*Bonjour!*" Amy said to Judy. Amy's group was doing France for their Around-the-World-in-Eight-Days project. "I like your lucky thumb ring! I have one too." She held out her hand.

"Same-same!" said Judy.

"Want to see my ABC gum collection?" Amy asked.

"Check!" said Judy.

"C'mon upstairs." Amy opened a funny-shaped door at the back of her room. It went to a small room under the stairs. "You have to duck or you'll bump your head," said Amy.

"Who lives here? Elves?" asked Judy.

"It's my secret place," said Amy. She pointed to the wall. Chewed-up gum was stuck all over the wall behind the staircase, where nobody could see.

"WHOA!" said Judy. "You've started your own Wall of Gum! Just like the one in California."

"Shh!" said Amy. "I don't want my mum to find out."

Judy pretended to zip her lips. "Zipper Lips!" said Amy, and they cracked up.

"Lipper Zipper!" said Judy, and they cracked up some more.

"Do you want your membership card?" asked Amy. "I sent away for it."

Amy handed the card to Judy. It looked way official. And it was signed by Hugh Blue, just like Amy's.

"Rare!" said Judy. "How did you get yours covered in plastic like that?"

"Sellotape!" said Amy. They taped up Judy's card to make it look even more official.

"It also comes with this stuff," said Amy.

Judy took the stuff out of the bag. There was a HI, MY NAME IS nametag, a My-Name-Is-a-Poem Club bike sticker, a list of members with rhyming names, from all over the world, and a game called the Name Game.

Judy and Amy played the Name Game. Judy made up rhyming names for Rocky, Frank and Jessica Finch. She made up eight names for Stink.

Stink McFink   Stinky Pinky
Stink LeWink   Stinky Blinky
Stinky Dinky   Stink the Shrink
Stink's a Jinx   Stink-a-Link

"Stink McFink is still the best," said Judy, laughing.

"Hey, I know," said Amy. "Let's write to some real people who rhyme."

"RARE!" said Judy. She took out her list.

"Just think," she said. "Now my name will be on the list one day. Judy Moody."

Amy got out a big plastic tub with all kinds of writing paper and smelly markers, coloured pencils, stickers, rubber stamps and glitter-glue pens.

"Blue glue!" said Judy.

"We can make our own postcards," said Amy. "I can even print some out on the computer. Then we can send them to other people in the club."

"OK," said Judy. "I'll send one to Larry Derry Berry, Viola Gazola, Yankee Pankee and Herman Sherman Berman. Can you believe there's a person in the club named T. Hee? No lie."

"T. Hee. That's funny," said Amy.

"Tee-hee-hee!" shouted Judy and Amy. They both cracked up.

Amy looked at the list. "I'll write to Lance France, Roos Van Goos, Pinky Dinky and Wong Fong from Hong Kong."

"You made that up," said Judy.

"Nope. It says so right here!" Judy and Amy fell on the floor, laughing some more.

Judy and Amy made postcards all morning. Judy wrote addresses on all her postcards till her hand almost fell off. "Finished!" she said.

"I've not finished yet," said Amy. "Why don't you do one more?"

"OK," said Judy. "How about Nathaniel Daniel? He's from the United States. San Luis Obispo, California."

"Let me see that!" said Amy. She looked
at the list. "That's where Bubblegum Alley
is. The real Wall of Gum. No lie."

"No way!" said Judy. "Let's send him
some gum and see if he'll stick it on the
wall for me. Then we can BOTH be on the
Wall of Gum."

"Okey-dokey!" said Amy.

"Let's break open the Make-Your-Own-Gum Kit I sent away for," said Judy. "I'm so glad I brought it. I've been dying to try it out. Now we can make our own gum to send him. Will it be OK with your mum?"

"Sure," said Amy. "As long as we clean up afterwards."

Judy and Amy went downstairs to the kitchen. "Let's have some lunch first," said Amy. "Mum left us ham and cheese sandwiches. I like to cut them up, like this." She took out some cookie cutters and the girls made sandwiches into stars, hearts, footballs, pumpkins and rabbits. Judy even made one of the United States (except Florida broke off).

Amy took the plate over to the table. "We'll never eat all these in a million years," said Judy.

"They're way more fun to make than to eat," said Amy, grinning at Judy with a milk moustache.

After lunch, Judy looked at her red watch. She looked at her purple watch. Which was which again? Wearing two watches could really get a person all mixed-up. But it was still early on BOTH watches.

"Do you have to go?" asked Amy.

"Nope. I have loads of time before I have to go to Rocky's to practise the tarantella dance," said Judy. "Let's get started!" She opened up the Make-Your-Own-Gum kit and pulled out a bag. "This must be the gum base. It's called chicle. It comes from the rainforest."

They poured bags of powder stuff and sticky stuff into a bowl. Then they melted it in the microwave.

"I need the mixing tool," said Judy.

They took turns mixing and stirring, mixing and stirring. Powder stuff flew up into the air and went everywhere. Sticky stuff stuck to the spoon and the chair and the table.

"Now for the fun part!" said Judy. They plopped a big sticky blob down onto some baking paper.

"It says to knead it like bread," said Amy.

"Dive in!" said Judy. They each took a big blob.

"Wait! We'd better take off all our watches," said Amy. "It's so sticky!"

"Icky, yicky, sticky!" said Judy.

"Ooey, gooey, chewy," said Amy.

Judy pushed back her hair. Judy scratched her nose. Judy dropped some on her knee.

"You've got gum all over you!" said Amy.

"So have you," said Judy. "Double bubble trouble!" They cracked up.

"Now for the best part," said Judy. "Flavours. They only give you two. Peppermint and tutti-frutti."

"We can make our own," said Amy.

"Like what?"

Amy looked in the cupboard. "Peanut-butter gum? Tuna-fish gum?"

"I don't think so!" said Judy.

Amy looked in the spice rack. "How about cinnamon gum? Vanilla gum? Rainbow-sprinkle gum?"

"Sure!" said Judy. "Why not!"

Amy looked in the refrigerator. "Ketchup gum? Mustard gum? Pickle gum?"

"That's it!" said Judy.

"Ketchup gum? Yick!"

"No!" said Judy. "Pickle gum." She poured some pickle from the jar and kneaded it into one of the blobs. "I can take some home to play a trick on Stink. He'll never know. I'll call it Pickle Chicle."

"A Pickle Chicle trick?" asked Amy.

"Exactly!" said Judy. "A Pickle Chicle trickle!"

They rolled and pressed and squeezed and stretched the gum until it was flat. Then they dusted it with icing sugar and cut it into pieces.

"Let's taste some," said Judy.

"Not the pickle gum, though," said Amy.

Judy popped one, two, three pieces of gum in her mouth. The gum stuck to her teeth. The gum stuck to her tongue. The gum stuck to the roof of her mouth.

"Is so sicky," said Judy.

"Sicky?" asked Amy.

"Stick-y!" said Judy. "My mouth feels like a hippo eating a jar of peanut butter!"

Amy popped one, two, three pieces in her mouth. Judy Moody and Amy Namey chewed and cracked and blew and popped gum until Judy's dad came and it was time to go.

She, Judy Moody, chewed her Peppermint Rainbow-Sprinkle Tutti-Frutti NOT Pickle-Chicle gum all the way home.

Pickle Chicle

"*Ciao!* I'm home!" called Judy as she walked through the door. Stink came pounding downstairs. When he saw Judy, his mouth dropped open.

"Stink? Are you trying to catch flies?" said Judy. "Your mouth's wide open."

He laughed and pointed. There was gum in her hair, gum on her nose, gum on her trousers, gum on her coat.

"What happened to you?" asked Stink. "Attack of the Killer Gumball?"

"Hardee-har-har, Stink. I was making gum at Amy Namey's with my Make-Your-Own-Gum Kit. It was way fun."

"Oh, you didn't wait for me?"

"No, but I made some special gum just for you. My own secret recipe." Judy opened up the wrapper and held out the gum for Stink to see.

He saw pink gum, brown gum, grey gum, green gum. And gum with lumps. "Eeuww! I'm not eating that lumpy, bumpy gum!"

"Yours is the green one," said Judy.

Stink picked up the green gum like he was picking up a worm.

"Just try it!" said Judy. "You'll like it!"
She blew a bubble and popped her own
gum.

Stink put the gum in his mouth. He
rolled it around on his tongue. He chewed
it. Once, twice.

"BLUCK!" said Stink, sticking out his tongue. "It's really sour. Worse than sourballs. What is this, anyway? Salt gum?"

"It's Pickle Chicle!" said Judy. "Get it? Pickle-flavoured gum! I made it with real pickle!"

"BLAH!" went Stink, spitting the gum across the room. Mouse pounced on it.

"Gross!" said Judy.

"Stink," said Dad, "pick that up and put it in the bin."

"Isn't Judy even in trouble? She tricked me with pickle gum!" said Stink.

"I think you'll live," said Dad.

"It probably had spider eggs in it!"

"Spider eggs?" said Judy.

"That's my fault," said Dad. "I was

telling Stink how when we were kids, there were all these rumours that gum had spider's eggs in it," said Dad. "We were actually afraid to chew gum."

"Weird!" said Judy.

"Speaking of spiders, guess what I got at Fur & Fangs!" said Stink.

"You mean Toady won the race?" asked Judy.

"Not exactly," said Stink. He held out a sandwich bag with a gross-looking spider skin in it. "It's a moulted spider."

"A melted spider?" asked Judy. "Gross!"

"Moul-ted. It's just the skin. Spiders have their skeleton on the outside, and they shed their skin to grow a new one."

"Rare," said Judy, peering into the bag.

"Toady wouldn't even hop once when it was time for the race. So the kid who won the tarantula gave it to me. I think he felt sorry for me."

"Tarantula!" cried Judy. "Holy macaroni! I was so busy at Amy's house, getting the scoop on the My-Name-Is-a-Poem Club and tricking you with pickle gum, that I forgot I was supposed to go to Rocky's! To practise the tarantula. I mean, the tarantella. Now *I'm* saying it."

"Here's a scoop for you," said Stink.

"Your friends aren't talking to you. I was supposed to tell you. Rocky called. And Frank called. Then Rocky called again. And that Jessica Finch person."

"Stink! Why didn't you tell me? What did they say?"

"They said to tell you that they're really mad you didn't show up and they are not doing the spider dance with you even if you pay them one million dollars."

"Judy, this sounds like a real mix-up," said Mum. "You were supposed to be working on a school project with Rocky and your other friends, but you were with Amy?"

"I didn't do it on purpose, Mum, and now they're mad and they'll never talk to me again."

"It'll work out, honey. Everybody makes mistakes," said Mum.

"We know you're excited about your new friend Amy," said Dad. "All we're saying is you need to take care not to forget about your old friends, too."

"I can't help it if they're mad," said Judy. "What can I say?"

"Just be honest," said Mum. "Tell them you lost track of time."

"Or tell them the Pickle Gum Monster took over your brain," said Stink.

"Yipes stripes!" Judy said. "I just can't believe this happened. I was getting all mixed up wearing two watches. Then I took off BOTH watches to wash my hands at Amy Namey's… I must have looked at the wrong one or something."

"So I guess you could say TWO watches AREN'T better than one!" said Stink.

No-Talky Rocky
vs
Judy Snooty

Judy called Rocky. "I'm sorry I'm late, but my two watches got me all mixed up and then I got attacked by a giant gumball and—"

"I'm not talking to you," said Rocky.

"You just did!" said Judy. "So you're NOT not talking to me!" She laughed. But Rocky did not crack up one teensy bit.

"I mean it," he told her. "Frank's mad too. He's already gone home. And Jessica

Finch doesn't even want to be in the group. She's making up her own Pizza Spelling Test."

"But we have to practise the dance! I'm coming over right now."

"Don't!" said Rocky. "I told you – I'm not talking to you."

"But I – we have to. You can't just—"

"*Hmm-hmm, hmm-hmm, hmm hmm hmm...*" Rocky would not listen. He just hummed "Twinkle, Twinkle, Little Star" into the phone.

Judy hung up the phone and went to find Stink. "You've got to come over to Rocky's with me," she said. "Now!"

"How come?"

"Because he's not talking to me."

"So?"

"So, he's NOT not talking to you."

❧　　❧　　❧

Judy ran across the street and rang the bell. She made Stink stand in front of her. Rocky opened the door.

ROCKY: Stink, tell Judy I said I'm not talking to her.

JUDY: Stink, please tell Rocky that we have to practise our dance.

STINK: Judy says you have to practise your dance.

ROCKY: Tell Judy that *she's* the one who didn't show up to practise. I don't want to dance like a spider anyway. I quit.

STINK: He quits.

JUDY: I heard. Please tell Rocky I had a really good excuse. Tell him about Attack of the Giant Gumball and everything.

STINK: She did get gum all over her. See? Look at her gummy hair.

ROCKY: Tell Judy too bad. It's too late. We waited till after three o'clock and Frank and Jessica Finch went home. And tell her we Q-U-I-T quit.

STINK: He Q-U-I-T quits.

JUDY: Stink, please tell Rocky he can't quit because if we don't do our project, we won't make it around the world in eight days.

Does he want to ruin it for
everybody? For Class 3V too?
Does he want us to F-L-U-N-K?

STINK: Do you want to flunk and ruin
it for everybody?

ROCKY: You've already ruined it. I mean,
tell Judy *she's* already ruined it.
If we flunk, it will be all her
fault.

STINK: Rocky says—

JUDY: Tell him I'm super, super sorry.
I got all mixed up with my two
watches because one was on
Italy time, but I'm here now,
aren't I?

ROCKY: Tell Judy it's not just about for-
getting the practice today.

She quit us, her best friends, for
Amy Rhymey. Tell her we can
rhyme too.

Rocky handed a piece of notebook
paper to Stink.

ROCKY: Here, read this.

JUDY: Read it, Stink. Let's hear it.

STINK: I think you should pay me
if I have to read stuff too.

JUDY: Just read it!

STINK: *My name is Frank.*

You can call me Frank the Tank.

When Judy didn't show up for practice,

It really stank.

ROCKY: Not that one. This one.

STINK: *My name is Rocky.*

I like hockey.

Really it's the only thing

That rhymes with Rocky.

I don't feel too talky.

Don't mean to be rudey –

I'm just mad at my friend

Judy Snooty.

STINK: Judy Snooty! That's a good one.

JUDY: Hardee-har-har.

STINK: Wait! There's one more:

My name is Stink.

I'm not a fink,

If that's what you think.

I just want some money—

JUDY: Stink! You just made that up.

ROCKY: Tell her Frank and I are quitting her.

JUDY: Fine.

ROCKY: Fine.

STINK: Judy's not doing the dance all by herself!

JUDY: Stink, tell Rocky I did not say that. I'll do the dance by myself.

STINK: You can't! How are you going to do a spider dance by yourself?

	A spider has eight legs! You need four people.
JUDY:	Stink! Just tell him.
STINK:	She'll do the dance by herself.
ROCKY:	Stink, ask her why doesn't she just get her New Best Friend, Amy Same-Samey, to do the dance with her?
STINK:	Ha! That's a good one! Judy, did you hear—
JUDY:	Ha, ha – so funny I forgot to laugh. Stink, please tell Rocky I can't do the dance by myself because he has the old record of the tarantella from his grandma. And tell him he has the old record player too.

ROCKY: Ha! So now you want to be friends again, huh? Because you need something.

STINK: Rocky says—

JUDY: Stink, ask Rocky, will he at least bring the stuff to school?

ROCKY: Um...

STINK: He said *um*.

JUDY: Um, he'll bring it? Or, um, he's thinking about it?

STINK: Rocky, what does *um* mean?

ROCKY: Um thinking! Get it?

STINK: I think he's thinking.

JUDY: Tell him I'm looking at BOTH my watches, and he has ten seconds. Nine, eight, seven—

ROCKY: Tell her I'll bring the record and

record player, but I won't do the
dance.

JUDY: Fine.

STINK: She said *fine*.

ROCKY: Fine.

STINK: He said *fine*.

JUDY: Fine.

STINK: I can't believe I'm not getting
         paid for this!

Elf Schmelf

First thing on Monday morning, when Judy got to school, she went to talk to Mr Todd.

"Mr Todd," said Judy, "you know how we're going around the world in eight days?"

"Yes," said Mr Todd.

"And you know how my group is supposed to be doing Italy?"

"Is there a problem?" asked Mr Todd.

"Sort of. I mean, yes. We can't do Italy. Or any country."

"I'm sorry to hear that," said Mr Todd. "Because not just our class, but Class 3V, too, is counting on going around the world in eight days. And we can't go around the world without Italy."

"It's sort of my fault," said Judy. "I missed a practice for the tarantella and Rocky and Frank and Jessica got mad and—"

"I'd like you to try to work this out yourselves," said Mr Todd. "Just do your best, OK?"

"I'll try," said Judy. "Jessica came up with something she'll do herself, but I know Rocky and Frank, and they can stay mad way longer than eight days."

"Well," said Mr Todd, "tell you what. How about if we visit Italy last? We can wait till Day Eight and do it at the very end."

"Thank you," said Judy. "Thank you, Mr Todd. I'll work it out. Or something."

❧   ❧   ❧

All week, Class 3T, along with Class 3V, had a blast going around the world. Judy tried to forget all about Rocky and Frank being mad at her. In England, Judy and Amy got to say "brilliant!". And they got to eat chips (aka French fries) with vinegar.

In France, Amy Namey led the two

classes in singing "Frère Jacques" in a round.

In Yeah Man (aka Yemen), they got to eat spicy beans and rice with their fingers! Then they got to try brushing their teeth with a stick, like Nellie Bly!

In Egypt, they built a giant sugar-cube pyramid. And in Japan, Judy got to try on a kimono and learn kirigami, the Japanese art of paper cutting. In China, they made brush paintings and ate fortune cookies (that were really from the Happy Garden Chinese Restaurant, not China!).

"What does your fortune say?" Judy asked Amy Namey.

You will find new friends soon.

"Nice!" said Judy.

"How about yours?" asked Amy. "What does it say?"

"Nothing," said Judy.

"It's blank? It has to say something. Let me see." Amy plucked the fortune right out of Judy's hand.

You will dance the tarantella ALONE.

"Don't worry!" said Amy. "It's not a real fortune! It's written on a sticky note. In kid handwriting."

"Something tells me it might just come true anyway," said Judy.

By the next Tuesday, Classes 3T and 3V had travelled the world for seven days. The next day was the last day. The next day was Day Eight. There was only one problem. Rocky and Frank were still M-A-D mad. Madder than a spider bite. Madder than a tarantula dancing the tarantella.

She, Judy Moody, was in a mood. She had a bad case of the DIY Blues. The Do-It-Yourself Blues. Judy always heard Mum and Dad saying "If you want to get something done, do it yourself". Maybe she *could* do the dance without Rocky and Frank. Jessica Finch, too. When Rocky and Frank saw how hard she'd worked on their Around-the-World project, she would save them from flunking and they wouldn't be mad any more.

So she, Judy Moody, official card-carrying member of the My-Name-Is-a-Poem Club, would make sure Classes 3T and 3V went around the world in eight days. She, Judy Moody, would DIH. Do. It. Herself.

Judy stayed up past bedtime reading about Italy and gluing pizza tables together and making up a game for everyone to play. She even made Stink practise the tarantella with her, but he just kept stomping on her feet.

When she woke up the next morning, Judy dressed in a red skirt and a green-and-white striped T-shirt. She even drew Italian flags on her white tights and wore her red shoes from the time she was Dorothy for Halloween.

"Who are you?" asked Stink. "One of Santa's elves?"

"Elf schmelf," said Judy. "Don't you know what's red, white and green all over?"

"Permanent markers that got on Mum's new white carpet?" asked Stink.

"I hope you're kidding," said Mum. "Hmm, let's see. Red, white and green. How about that strange spaghetti Dad makes?"

"I thought you liked my tri-colour pasta," said Dad. "You said it was creative!"

"It's creative all right," said Mum, making a funny face.

"Well, I hope we're not having that tonight," said Judy. "Because I borrowed lots of pasta for my Pasta Shapes Game."

"OK, so tell me," said Dad. "What's red, white and green all over? A Christmas zebra?"

"No-o!" said Judy. "It has nothing to do with Christmas."

"I know!" said Stink. "How about the flag of Bulgaria, Hungary, Mexico or Madagascar?"

"Mad-at-what-car? Hello! How about It-a-ly, Stink? The flag of Italy is red, white and green."

"I can't help it. I haven't read the *I* volume of the encyclopedia yet," said Stink. "Besides, you don't look like a flag. And I should know. I was a human flag once…"

"Wow, this must be quite a project," said Dad.

"It is," said Judy. "It took Nellie Bly seventy-two days to go around the world, and she beat the record. Try going around the whole world in just eight days!"

"So, have you patched things up with your friends now?" asked Mum.

"It's still a little rocky," said Judy. "But after today—"

"A little *Rocky*? Get it?" asked Stink.

"Ha, ha," said Judy. "Stink, can I borrow your tarantula skeleton to take to school? And your tambourine?"

"I don't know," said Stink. "I'll think about it."

"Stink, don't be a *bratellino*. Not today. Please."

"Do they have a lot of tarantulas and tambourines in Italy or something?" asked Stink.

"Or something," said Judy.

"No, I mean it," said Stink.

"Stink, for a kid who reads the encyclopedia, you don't really know much."

"I haven't read the *T* volume yet either!" said Stink.

"Well, you'd better get cracking!" said Judy. "Didn't you know? In the country of Italy, tarantulas play the tambourine while eating tortellini!"

Red-White-and-Green Machine

When Judy got to school that morning, she bumped into Amy Namey in the corridor.

"I can't wait to hear about Italy!" said Amy. "We get to come over to your class again. I can't wait to see your group do that spider dance!"

"*I'm* my group," said Judy. She stepped into Class 3T and stood the Leaning Tower of Pizza Tables on the shelf by the window.

She covered it with an upside-down box so nobody would see till later.

"Rocky, did you bring the record? And the record player?" asked Judy.

"Frank," said Rocky, "tell Judy I brought the record player."

"Yipes stripes! You're still not talking to me?" asked Judy.

Rocky zipped his lips.

"Lipper Zipper," said Judy, cracking herself up.

"Huh?" asked Frank.

"Never mind," said Judy. "You had to be there. And I was. With Amy Namey. Not you two!"

As soon as the bell rang, it was time for Judy's group to talk about Italy. Judy and Jessica stood up in front of Class 3T and Class 3V.

"Judy," asked Mr Todd, "what about the rest of your group?"

"C'mon, you guys," Judy whispered.

Rocky and Frank came and stood at the front. "Um, Rocky's having trouble with his voice or something," said Judy. "So I'll be talking for my group. Frank will hold up the flag of Italy." Judy handed the flag to Frank.

"*Ciao*, everybody," said Judy. "First, Jessica Finch will hand out a Pizza Spelling Test."

"Test!?" everybody complained.

"It's just for fun," said Jessica. "And you can do it whenever you want. It's not like it's H-O-M-E-W-O-R-K or anything."

"Now," said Judy Moody, "first I'll tell you a little about Italy. Then we'll play a game and I'll show you a dance. So, Italy has some really funny-sounding cities. Like Baloney, Italy. And Pizza, Italy."

"It's Ba-LON-ya," said Mr Todd. "And PEE-za, Italy."

"Bravo!" said Judy. "In the town of Pizza, there's this tower, but it's crooked. So it's called the Leaning Tower of Pizza."

"And guess what?" said Jessica Finch. "If you mess up the letters in THE LEAN-ING TOWER OF PISA, you get WHAT

A FOREIGN STONE PILE. It's called an anagram."

"Anyway," said Judy, "I made a leaning tower to show you what it looks like."

"That was our idea!" said Rocky.

"Rocky, I see you've found your voice," said Mr Todd.

"This was Rocky and Frank's idea," said Judy. *"Voilà!"*

"*Voilà* is French," said Jessica Finch. "We learned that last week."

"May I present," said Judy, "the Leaning Tower of Pizza Tables." She yanked off the box.

Something wasn't right! The Leaning Tower of Pizza Tables wasn't leaning at all.

It was *melted*. What used to be a leaning stack of glued-together pizza tables was now just a great big globby blob of melty plastic.

"Ahhh!" Everybody pointed and cracked up.

"I'm melting!" said Rocky in a Wicked-Witch-of-the-West voice.

"Oh, no!" said Judy. "My Leaning Tower of Pizza Tables. I put it on the shelf ... above the radiator!"

"The heat melted them," said Rocky.

"We'll just have to call it the Melted Tower of Pizza," said Frank.

"Don't feel bad," said Amy Namey. "That's like what happened to my papier-mâché globe. Globe explode! Remember?"

"OK, folks, the show must go on!" said Mr Todd.

Judy took out the supplies for the Pasta Shapes Game.

"Everybody gets their own board and a little bag with pasta in it," said Judy, holding up a bag and rattling it. "You match the different kinds of pasta in the bag with the shapes on your board."

"Great idea," said Mr Todd.

"That sounds like lots of fun," said Ms Valentine.

"Then write the name of the pasta under it. If you don't know the name, you can look at my chart." Judy held up a piece of cardboard that had pasta shapes glued onto it. Above each kind of pasta was its name.

PASTAS FROM ITALY		
CAPPellini	Penne	elbowmacaroni
FARfalle	Rotini	fettuccine
spaghetti	fusilli	Linguine
Vermicelli	Pastina	Ziti
ravioli	Tortellini	Pappardelle

Everybody cracked up. "Ha, ha!" Bradley pointed.

"You're missing some," said a kid from the other class.

"Where's the elbow macaroni?" somebody asked.

"And the vermicelli? And the cappellini?" asked Jessica.

Judy stared at her cardboard. How could she have missed any? She had even stayed up late making sure she had every single last one glued into place.

She marched over to Rocky and Frank. "Which one of you stole them? Give them here." She held out her hand.

"I didn't do anything! Honest!" said Rocky.

Frank was chewing away on something. And the something was not gum. The something was pasta shapes from her game.

"You ate them!?" cried Judy.

"I got hungry just standing here being a flag," mumbled Frank.

"Eeuw! Use your noodle, Frank," she said, pointing to her head. "Those pasta shapes were not even cooked!"

"So?" said Frank. "They still taste good."

"Yuck!" said Judy. "They had GLUE on them. I'm going to tell the whole world that you, Frank Pearl, ate glue."

"So? Everybody thinks I eat paste anyway."

"ROAR-a-lini!" said Judy.

❧ ❧ ❧

The Leaning Tower of Pizza Tables had melted. The Pasta Shapes Game had been eaten. Getting around the world in eight days was definitely not easy.

But nothing would wreck the tarantella. Nothing. It had to be perfect. If only she hadn't forgotten about the practice that day. Now she, Judy Moody, would dance the tarantella alone. Just like her fortune had said.

Rocky would play the record. Frank would shake the tambourine. And Jessica Finch would clap along.

She could not mess this up, or half the class would be mad that they hadn't made it around the world in eight days.

While everyone finished the Pasta Shapes Game, Mr Todd pushed desks and stuff into the corner so Judy would have plenty of room.

"Okey-dokey," said Judy. "This morning I am going to dance the tarantella."

"The tarantula?" somebody asked.

"No, not the tarantula," said Frank.

"Well, actually, you're never going to believe it, but I looked it up. Did you know *tarantella* means 'tarantula'. For real and absolute positive. My dad told me the dance started a long time ago, before he was even born, around the Middle Ages." Mr Todd and Ms Valentine cracked up.

Judy held up the tarantula skin in a bag. Everybody squirmed. "EEUW!"

"Don't worry, it's not a real spider. Just the skin or the skeleton of a tarantula. Anyway, this dance is called the Spider Dance. Some people say it started because if you got bitten by a tarantula, then you'd act like a loon and dance to get all the spider-bite stuff out of your system. A doctor even wrote about it and said this dance was a cure for spider bites."

"Interesting," Mr Todd said, raising his eyebrows.

"A spider has eight legs, so usually you need four people," said Judy, glancing over at Rocky, Frank and Jessica.

"Judy," said Mr Todd, "why don't you show us? Then we'll call on some others to come up and try it with you."

"*Fantastico!*" said Judy. Rocky started the record. Judy faced the class. She stretched her hands in the air. Frank started to shake the tambourine. Jessica Finch clapped. Judy took a deep breath. "Nice and easy," she told herself.

Da da da, duh da da da,

Da da da-da-da-da-duh

Step-hop, slide. Step-hop, slide. Change step. Hop. Skip. Slap knee. Repeat. Buzz turn. Spin in place.

"One, two, three and four," Judy counted to herself. She tried to remember all the steps she'd practised. She tried to remember to reverse direction when the music changed. She tried to keep up with the music as it got faster.

Stephopslide. Stephopslide. Change!
Step! Hop! Skip! Slapknee! Repeat!

Da da da, duh da da da,

Da da da-da-da-da-duh

Something wasn't right! The music was too fast!

Judy made her feet go faster and faster until her head was dizzy and her hair was in her mouth.

"Too – *puff puff* – fast!" she panted. "Slow – *puff puff* – down!" *Huff puff puff.*

But nobody seemed to hear. The music kept getting faster and faster. Frank shook the tambourine faster than an earth-quake. Judy whirled and twirled, a dizzy dancing dervish. Her feet were moving so fast, she felt like a spider with eight legs.

The class was clapping and shouting and laughing and pointing. Mr Todd flicked the lights on and off. Judy spun like a top out of control – a dizzy, dancing, red-white-and-green machine!

Suddenly, she banged into a desk, tripped over her own foot and fell in a red-white-and-green heap on the floor.

"Oops. Was it too fast?" Rocky asked innocently.

"*Stupido!*" Judy mumbled.

She, Judy Moody, knew that Rocky and Frank had revved up the tarantella music on purpose.

It was just plain red, white and mean.

Eatsa Pizza

The tarantella had turned out to be a big fat flop. Nobody with *two* legs could dance as fast as a spider with *eight* legs. Now they would never make it around the world in eight days. And everybody would blame her, even though she had danced her legs off!

She, Judy Moody, had flunked.

It was all Rocky and Frank's fault. Rocky No-Talky and Frank the Prank. The My-Name-Is-NOT-a-Poem Club.

After Class 3V left the room, Mr Todd had a private talk with Judy, Rocky, Frank and Jessica. He talked to them about what it means to work together as a group. He wanted them to work out their differences, to give each other a second chance. He wanted them to be friends again. But most of all, *he* wanted to give *them* a second chance.

"Do I have to have a second chance?" asked Jessica. "Because I think I tried to be a T-E-A-M P-L-A-Y-E-R."

"You know," said Mr Todd, "in Italy there's a saying. 'You can't make an omelette without breaking eggs.'"

"For real?" said Judy.

"Absolutely," said Mr Todd. "Things

often go wrong before they go right. It happens all the time."

"I've heard of 'break a leg' but never 'break an egg'," said Jessica.

"Boys, how about I give you until tomorrow morning to do your part for our Around-the-World project?" Mr Todd said.

"You mean we can still think up our own Italy project and bring it in tomorrow morning?" asked Rocky.

"And then we'd still get to go around the world, even though it took eight and a half days?" asked Frank.

"I don't see why not," said Mr Todd. "Even Nellie Bly had a lot of things go wrong on her trip around the world."

"Yeah, like there was a bad storm and she almost didn't make it back to America on time," said Jessica.

"And McGinty, her monkey, got scared and jumped on a lady's back!" said Judy. "Everybody said he was bad luck and wanted Nellie to throw him overboard!"

"That's right," said Mr Todd. "So, what do you say? Does it sound like a plan?"

"It's a plan," said Rocky and Frank.

Rocky turned to Judy. "We're sorry you did all the work and for messing up your dance," said Rocky. "You were REALLY fast! So fast it looked like you had eight legs!"

"And we're sorry for eating your Pasta Shapes Game and for getting mad," said Frank. "We really messed up."

"I messed up, too," said Judy. "I'm the one who missed our practice. All I could think about was the My-Name-Is-a-Poem Club, and I guess I forgot my old friends." She held out a hand. Rocky and Frank piled their hands on top of hers.

"Don't forget me!" said Jessica, adding her hand to the top of the pile.

๏   ๏   ๏

Magnifico! Fantastico! Judy could not wait to tell Amy Namey that Classes 3T and 3V were going to go around the world in eight (and a half) days after all!

Rocky and Frank had to think up a project. Fast. And Judy and Jessica did not even have to help. Mr Todd said the boys needed to work it out all by themselves.

"So what are you going to do?" Judy asked them.

"It's a surprise," said Frank.

"It's a really big scoop," said Rocky.

"Well, it'd better not be the Leaning

Tower of Pizza Tables again, because half my collection has melted."

"It'll be better," said Frank.

"It'll be big," said Rocky.

"It'll be red, white and green!" said Rocky and Frank, cracking themselves up.

"Is it ... the Grinch ... on a fire engine?" Jessica guessed.

"You'll see," said Rocky.

"You'll see," said Frank.

"Break an egg!" said Judy.

The next morning, Rocky was not on the bus. And Judy was dying to show him the letter and photo she'd received from Nathaniel Daniel in California.

When Judy got to school, she ran straight to Amy's class.

"Look what I've got!" she told Amy Namey.

"It's Bubblegum Alley!" said Amy.

"Look closer," Judy said.

Amy peered at the photo and found the initials *JM* made out of chewed-up gum.

"*JM* for *Judy Moody*! I'm on the Wall of Gum!" said Judy. "In the Bubblegum Hall of Fame."

"Double check!" said Amy.

ⓔ　ⓔ　ⓔ

"Hey, have you seen Rocky? Or Frank?" Judy asked Jessica Finch when she got to class.

"Didn't you hear? The two of them got here super early and they've been down in the canteen all morning. I can't wait to find out what they're up to." The whole class was buzzing about the big scoop. Rocky and Frank even got to miss Spelling.

Finally, Rocky and Frank came back upstairs. They told Mr Todd and Ms Valentine to bring everybody down to the canteen in five minutes.

"What *IS* it?" asked Judy, rushing up to Rocky and Frank.

"We're not telling!" they said.

Class 3T and Class 3V walked single file along the corridor and down the stairs to the canteen. They could smell it before they saw it. Everybody had a seat at one of the lunch tables.

The project was so big, it would not fit through the door, so the dinner ladies had to help them slide it through the hatch from the kitchen. In came a dinner lady, then Rocky, then Frank, then another dinner lady. They were holding their hands over their heads and carrying the biggest, roundest circle of cardboard Judy had ever seen.

"YUM!" said Jessica Finch.

"Smells good!" said Judy.

"What is it?" everybody asked.

It took six pushed-together tables just to hold it. They set the cardboard down. On it was the biggest, bubbliest, yummiest, cheesiest pizza in the world.

"What's red, white and green all over?" asked Frank.

"The World's Biggest Pizza!" Rocky announced. "Red sauce and white cheese with green-pepper topping!"

"No way!" everybody said.

"Yah-huh," said Rocky. "At least, it's Virginia Dare School's Biggest-Ever Pizza. It's two metres wide, and we used fourteen kilos of dough and sixteen kilos of cheese."

"That pizza weighs more than me!" shouted Judy.

"Actually," said Frank, "the real World's Biggest Pizza is about the size of a car park."

"But this *is* the World's Biggest Pizza *Map!*" said Rocky.

"What? Huh?"

Everybody gathered around the pizza and took a closer look. It was as big and round as the world, and the cheese was piled in seven funny shapes. One for each continent. Like a map! Green peppers made a trail from North America to the tip of Asia.

"I get it! It's a map!"

"It's the world!"

"I see North America!"

"I see Italy! It's the shape of a boot," said Judy.

"Look!" said Amy Namey. "The pizza map follows Nellie Bly's trip around the world."

"Right – it's all the places we went around the world in eight and a half days," said Judy.

Amy Namey took out her clipboard. "I'm going to be first to get the big scoop," she told Judy. "I'll write this up for my newspaper! WORLD'S BIGGEST PIZZA MAP AT VIRGINIA DARE SCHOOL."

"Don't forget CLASS 3T AND 3V GO AROUND THE WORLD IN EIGHT AND A HALF DAYS!" said Judy.

"Eight and a half days, two hours, thirteen minutes and twenty-seven seconds," said Amy, looking at both her watches.

"Check!" said Rocky and Frank, sounding like Amy Namey.

"*Fantastico!*" said Judy.

"Dig in!" said a dinner lady. "There's more than enough for everybody."

"There's more than enough to have pizza for lunch every day for a week!" said Rocky.

"Pizza for lunch every day? Told you that could happen," said Amy Namey.

Magnifico!

Judy and Rocky and Frank and Amy each picked up a slice. A string of ooey-gooey cheese stretched from Rocky's to Frank's to Judy's to Amy's slice of pizza.

"Hey! We're all connected!" said Judy.

"The Eatsa Pizza Club!" said Frank.

"Double cool," said Rocky.

"Triple yum," said Frank.

"Quadruple check!" said Amy Namey.

And the four friends laughed themselves red, white and green all over. Then they sat down and ate the biggest, cheesiest, most *delizioso* pizza in the world.

For sure and absolute *positivo*!

The *whole world's* in a Judy Moody mood!

Say hello to . . .

Fleur Humeur (Judy Moody in the Netherlands)

 or Dada Nalada (Judy Moody in Slovakia)

or Hania Humorek (Judy Moody in Poland).

The Judy Moody series has been published in more than twenty countries and languages, for a grand total of more than **12 million books** in print worldwide.

Open up a book – anywhere, any-time – and get ready for your *best mood ever*!

Have you read them all?

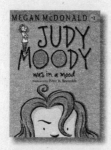

MEGAN McDONALD
JUDY MOODY
was in a mood
Illustrated by Peter H. Reynolds

MEGAN McDONALD
JUDY MOODY
Gets Famous!
Illustrated by Peter H. Reynolds

MEGAN McDONALD
JUDY MOODY
Saves the World!
Illustrated by Peter H. Reynolds

MEGAN McDONALD
JUDY MOODY
Predicts the Future
Illustrated by Peter H. Reynolds

MEGAN McDONALD
JUDY MOODY
The Doctor Is In!
Illustrated by Peter H. Reynolds

MEGAN McDONALD
JUDY MOODY
Declares Independence!
Illustrated by Peter H. Reynolds

MEGAN McDONALD
JUDY MOODY
Around the World in 8½ Days
Illustrated by Peter H. Reynolds

MEGAN McDONALD
JUDY MOODY
Goes to College
Illustrated by Peter H. Reynolds

MEGAN McDONALD
JUDY MOODY
Girl Detective
Illustrated by Peter H. Reynolds

Judy Moody's
ALL YOU NEED IS A PENCIL!
Double-Rare
Way-Not-Boring
Book of
Fun Stuff to Do
Megan McDonald Illustrated by Peter H. Reynolds

Judy Moody's
Way Wacky
Uber Awesome
Book of
More Fun Stuff to Do
Megan McDonald Illustrated by Peter H. Reynolds

THE
Judy Moody
MOOD
JOURNAL
Megan McDonald
Illustrated by Peter H. Reynolds

10 Things You May Not Know About Megan McDonald

10. The first story Megan ever got published (in the fifth grade) was about a pencil sharpener.

9. She read the biography of Virginia Dare so many times at her school library that the librarian had to ask her to give somebody else a chance.

8. She had to be a boring-old pilgrim every year for Halloween because she has four older sisters, who kept passing their pilgrim costumes down to her.

7. Her favourite board game is the Game of Life.

6. She is a member of the Ice-Cream-for-Life Club at Screamin' Mimi's in her hometown of Sebastopol, California.

5. She has a Band-Aid collection to rival Judy Moody's, including bacon-scented Band-Aids.

4. She owns a jawbreaker that is bigger than a baseball, which she will never, ever eat.

3. Like Stink, she had a pet newt that slipped down the drain when she was his age.

2. She often starts a book by scribbling on a napkin.

1. And the number-one thing you may not know about Megan McDonald is: she was once the opening act for the World's Biggest Cupcake!

10 Things You May Not Know About Peter H. Reynolds

10. He has a twin brother, Paul. Paul was born first, fourteen minutes before Peter decided to arrive.

9. Peter is part owner of a children's book and toy shop called the Blue Bunny in the Massachusetts town where he lives.

8. He's vertically challenged (aka short!).

7. His mother is from England; his father is from Argentina.

6. He made his first animated film while he was in high school.

5. He sometimes paints with tea instead of water – whatever's handy!

4. He keeps a sketch pad and pen on his nightstand. That way, if an idea hits him in the middle of the night, he can jot it down immediately.

3. His favourite candy is a tie between peanut-butter cups and chocolate-covered raisins (same as Megan McDonald!).

2. One of his favourite books growing up was *The Tall Book of Make-Believe* by Jane Werner, illustrated by Garth Williams.

1. And the number-one thing you may not know about Peter H. Reynolds is: he shares a birthday with James Madison, Stink's favourite president!

DOUBLE RARE!

Judy Moody has her own
interactive website!

Visit **www.judymoody.com** for all things
Judy Moody and lots of way-not-boring
fun stuff, including:

- ❂ The Official Judy Moody Fan Club

- ❂ Interactive games and a Mood Meter

- ❂ Way-not-boring stuff about Megan McDonald
  and Peter H. Reynolds

- ❂ Digital downloads, including emoticons and
  wallpapers

- ❂ Sample chapters and downloadable reading logs

Be sure to check out Stink's adventures too!

Judy and Stink are starring together!

Judy Moody and Stink
The Holly Joliday

Judy Moody and Stink
The Mad, Mad, Mad, Mad
Treasure Hunt

In full colour!